The Terrible
Topsy-Turvy,
Tissy-Tossy Tangle

Lily Whisker was a famous inventor.
Day and night, she was busy
with her inventing.

One day,
she invented a mysterious potion
that made things whizz and fizz.

"What else does it do?"
asked her twin brother Lionel Whisker,
the famous spaghetti cook.

"It whizzes and fizzes," Lily said.
"That's enough to go on with."
She put a cross on the label of the bottle.

They did not know
that Iris La Bonga, the famous spy,
was listening at the open window
with her spy's hearing trumpet.

"Aha!" said Iris.
"I must steal this mysterious potion
as soon as possible."

She ran off to her spy's van
to put on a clever disguise.

Lionel Whisker said to his sister,
"It's all very well to invent mysterious potions
but why don't you invent a new tomato sauce?
We are having spaghetti for lunch."

"We always have spaghetti," complained Lily,
but she loved inventing.
In half an hour she had invented
a completely new tomato sauce.
She put a letter 'T' on the label.

"Here's that tomato sauce you wanted,"
Lily said to Lionel.

Lionel came to get the sauce.
"Terrific!" he said, picking up the wrong bottle.
He took the wrong bottle into the kitchen.
He emptied the wrong bottle
into his best, big, blue pot of spaghetti.

"My word, what a whizzing and fizzing!"
he said, frowning.

Just then there was a knock at the door.
Lionel opened it.
There was Iris La Bonga, the famous spy.
She was disguised as a dear little girl.

"I've lost my mother!"
she said, pretending to cry.

"What a dear little girl!" said Lionel.
"Come into the kitchen.
I will ring the Society for Finding Lost Mothers."

Iris was left alone in the kitchen.

"What's this I see?"
muttered the wicked Iris.
"A bottle with a cross on it!
What luck! I'll take it now."

As Iris put out her hand,
something whizzed and fizzed.
Something bumped in the big blue pot.

"What's in that pot?" wondered Iris.

Bumpity, bump, bump, bump,
went the lid of the big blue pot,
as though something was trying to get out.

Iris just had to have a look.
Spies are like that.

Iris opened the pot.

Out leaped a great, big, terrible
topsy-turvy, tissy-tossy tangle.
The spaghetti had come alive.
It looked like white spiders wrestling.
It looked like twenty octopuses dancing
on top of one another.

"What a dear little girl!"
it cried in a slippery voice.

Iris screamed.
She ran as fast as she could
back to her spy's van.

The terrible topsy-turvy, tissy-tossy tangle
went running after her.
It leaped up on the roof of the van.

When Iris La Bonga drove off
the terrible topsy-turvy, tissy-tossy tangle
went with her.

Lionel came out into the kitchen.

"What's this?" he cried.
"That dear little girl
has wolfed down all my spaghetti
and run away.
Well, this is the last time
I help a dear little girl
who has lost her mother."

Then Lionel said to Lily,
"The spaghetti has gone.
We'll have to eat fish and chips instead."

Lily Whisker went on with her inventing.
Much to her surprise,
she won a great big science award
for a new sort of tomato sauce.

That made her even more famous.

As for Iris La Bonga,
she is still trying to get away
from the terrible topsy-turvy, tissy-tossy tangle.
And it is still tumbling after her.

Serves her right!

It just shows—
you should always read a label
very, very carefully.